paint it black

MANIMESH KR BORSAIKIA

AF518109

BlueRose ONE.com
Stories Matter
NewDelhi • London

BLUEROSE PUBLISHERS
India | U.K.

For permissions requests or inquiries regarding this publication, please contact:

BLUEROSE PUBLISHERS
www.BlueRoseONE.com
info@bluerosepublishers.com
+91 8882 898 898
+4407342408967

ISBN: 978-93-7139-436-9

Cover Design: Aman Sharma
Typesetting: Pooja Sharma

First Edition: June 2025

Bright eyed were the colors but unfortunate was the statue , too early to fall down , too early to touch a clown , a glass in the dark , pretended to be invisible , pretended to be unbreakable, dry was the touch , shy was the brush , to paint it all black. Seriousness aside doing all the stupid things, an intelligent one brings and Isha was intelligent, whatever the leftover brings, , bring me a piece , Isha cried, bring me a dish , bring me a fish , doesn't it get hurt , she asked. To get fried, were you shouting when they cried, were you worried when he died, seriousness aside doing all the stupid things. Inapproachable were the first rates, rates on rich plates, rich food on slates , honesty left to fate, Isha didn't hate, times she rarely spoke, times Isha rarely woke , some reason to add , a season still silent, times when she looks up and dreams are bare . Woke up to reality, has she or still dreaming , is it still happening, hard truth of love, sad truth of love , sad truth of being fake, hard truth of being awake..... seriousness aside.....

He wasn't asked to do something, something somewhere he felt though as he was writing, a kind of magic on paper ,shuttlecocks didn't interest Shahid , he was born ulta some said , the ass came before or the head only, the doctors and nurses knew, but who remembers....People remember the firsts for example , the first prime minister and the second , hardly, hit me hard, hit me soft from the back Isha said in her sleep. Sleep induced from pills, a life not on the hills, no light no bills, you would love that Shahid said, the one who was born ulta-pulta but Isha found it hard to go anywhere far from her rajma chawal stand, that was what Delhi did, a kind of secret powder that went into the chollez and rajmas and tongues would lick them endlessly, nothing less, nothing more......

Reading history huh! What kind of story, it's history, banished into the snow flakes , the fur was containing the heat in between the wet sheets, do you feel the chill of the wet sheets, Shahid wasn't in search of a story or for that matter history. Lights were lighting the ancient portrait of a man being nailed and those far away sails of cries...alas...Isha was a stiff young woman who was stiff in her voice , unusual in her choice, still water was playing in the dark but she preferred the lark as the early sunrise brought hopes , not for the one who didn't want to see but observe into the wall of judgement, judging your sail of cries, your shame , your name, your fame. Isha wasn't loyal to anyone or maybe everyone but her words , the far away lands she could go to hammer her own words and still there was a lingering doubt , do I need to go so far , do I need to prove , do I need the needy. Questions galore and Isha preferred the silence within.

Tribute of the pictures , hang one on my heart so that a hole could be dug with hands so he could bury his love , not the dead , not the living , but his love within. Ashni was listening to a story and a while later she realized her's wasn't any different. And the terrible night echoes so one hand reached the other, how many died in these hands , all's she, all's thee .....

Looking at the blooming rose, rose in an air of change , a laugh with a heartache , obligation of boredom, meanwhile it kind of bored Shahid , and also bothered him , why don't you write letters , better at the fretters, letters to the maters, looking at the blooming rose.

Shloka: Did you leave the keys at the watchmen

Isha: We got to do that

Shloka: We got to lock doors

Isha: But don't we have smart doors

Shloka: Not yet

Isha: Hai Ram! What's the point of owning such a big house

Shloka: Ask pappu

Isha: Pappu's always busy

Shloka: I got to go later to a party

Isha: But you ain't dressed that way

Shloka: I will just put on a tee

Isha: Shouldn't we sell those brands at our stores

Shloka: don't you talk about business now

Isha: but.....

Shloka: You could think a bit about charity too you know

Isha: I am charitable enough

Shloka: well ....how

Isha : with my lips

Shloka: what ?

Isha: There's enough roaming around to lick it

Shloka: Cheee.....cheee.... How dirty you talk

Isha : oh! Sweety ....you should hear when I drink

Shloka: I need a coffee , my head's hurting

Isha: I took a pill in Ibiza for my head

Shloka: No.....

Isha : oh! Yes

Isha : I woke up beside a group of naked men

Shloka: That's crazy

Isha : Yup ..... A bit.....

Shloka : And did you use .....

Isha : What ? Condoms???....

Shloka looked shocked

Shloka didn't talk further and looked out of the window.....

How willing was the affection, affectionate for that matter, a latte for later, commissions did try to meet her , innocent was willing ,cooking and drilling, undertook the billing, transmissions on request , until the sack wore out, facts that came out , recollection became collection, suggestions to a nation , how willing was the affection.

Pleasure of the distance , a distance that kept away , a distance that kept strange, shaking were contrarian thoughts , affections of a melted state , do you like melted chocolate better?

Or melted cream?

Reading to the disappointed , disappointed on beliefs , an old gal on search ,trying to get away , trying to get strange , pleasure of the distance.....

Rumors had nothing to do with mystery , toasted a slice of the blind history, apprehensive was the grand piper, it was a childhood dream of Shahid to be a grand piper, , shopping windows of the viper, millions of leaves vanished under the belt of trade winds . A pause to begin , a loss to begin. Musing amidst the rocks was Isha . Illness, a house stock. Awfully dull was Mazdock , tick tock, tick tock. ......

The afternoon was silent but the stove was burning. Avni wanted clear air and she let loose her hair , isn't boiled water fair king lair . Boiling water with leaves on top, some crushed , some curled. An inexpensive one at that . Hot chocolate for Lennie , finding Mrs. Fanny. Sailing with exciting lives , lighting and reading lives , wife of the wives , queen of the hives. " What's bad in it , to dream to be a queen" , Avni asked herself . It just wasn't a mirror but a glass that talked to her sometimes. But this time reply was none.....

A Dickensian way of life, happens to be on Tina Badi's visit, happens to be on Tina's list , she is fussy over her list, a five year old fist , tried hard to carry the worldly burden, downeth by the fathre, downeth by the mothre, scoring points against all ego, tolerating all idiocy, tolerating all crazy , a Dickensian way of life. Is it all worth it....Reading a book, the book came out of it's covers and welded a magic upon her, she a little girl not of little shape and size but who gave little importance to dreams , Shloka was much attracted to facts and real things . " Things to disown , dreams not my own

What not the world has shown

Blown often out of proportion

Bozo and Gozo in motion"

" Oh ! Shit ! I could miss my bus" , Shloka often missed her 602 bus on the outer ring road that took her to Jhunjhunwala Aptech classes.

< Hello Python >

Only that much of a language had Shloka learned in her language classes. She was more interested if Python would come out and reveal all the secrets of the IT world to her . She feared that . She wouldn't like to hear other people's secrets and sometimes she would close her eyes when the teacher gave any command.

< Python reveal >

Oh! Shit!.......

Where did you leave the orphan, was it your big purse or in the hands of the dying nurse , looked and paused a room, image of a gloom, great amazement in doom, passion and modesty, structurally made , ain't you. I can't probe you, I can't prove you, you are so strong on probity or were you playing nobility....side crossing civility ....

" I am out , out of the door , out of the deal , out of the feel", Mark wasn't looking for the right products but something that had a connection, but connection sucks, believed Mark, he had more of that than anyone else. Then he was in the bed snoring last night's beer off . Fresh was the sun, fresh was the banana, a banana that could call, really for what, to be bananas, to look bananas, or what do you expect the Americans doing , building bananas, oh we have loads of them , natural and fresh , thank God for bananas......

Ten thousand eyes were looking into the stage artist . Everyday the actor would stay there , act , drink , spill ,cry , laugh and then sleep . Earlier there was no one . Slowly and steadily the crowd noticed his skills in narration. There was some craft how Anand M. used to do it. Anand was protesting with placard in hands about the gender discrimination in Olympics. Anand held his hand in his dick and showcased manpower fighting against breasts and pussies. Russies were behind that , ban then , ban the Russians and the man pussies. People clapped , Anand bowed in tears ......

The sun wasn't clear and the elephants tried to hide their trunk. Nearby was Kawatani showcasing her newly born eagle to the Jungle world. The tigress was trying to climb the tree and the tree was feeling vulnerable between the gamblers of the eco system and the foxes . Foxes were cunning and would take you by surprise on the hunt. Kawatani also had her old tigress Hosana by her side who protected her from all kinds of evil. The throne wasn't in danger but rains could play foul . Kawatani was playing a secret magic school for the jungle life and it's inhabitants. But Mochu Pichu wouldn't allow it . For them , if the animals knew the secrets of man , it meant red , it meant danger and blood. Kawatani thought it was time to call up for the arrival of man ......

How serious was the inflation, deflation, really, both are opposite, both hurts basically says Kishore- liberals ,right wings, leftists whatever says kishore. Kishore didn't look at macroeconomics he looked at the sun and thought he could harness the flaming fire and then fire the unlit streets of villages of India . Play the proxy, play the foxy , there is demand oh oh hohoohhoho..... There is lot of demand. Could you then store electricity? Yes in my head jackass ...and then transfer it to all the heads of state . Then the thinking would come . But how to harness the sun's power . Shut up and don't ask , I am listening to Ariana , that miniature of sexiness, Yes And?

There were some curls and some furls twigs and swigs , men and women showing off their bodies , body is the problem, isn't it , fat , slim heavy , light , dark , white , Avni though liked white. Avni wanted the earth to be full of whites. She hated black . If she could she would have ...mm.... Couldn't say it , couldn't write, only fight , fight the black . Protesting was boring to her , picketing was old fashioned so Avni chose to limestone all the buildings white in the night . Ahh!!! Finally the city looks clean , Avni said with a clear sigh and relief.... Mani couldn't take it easy . He couldn't take it lightly and so licked the latrine where Avni's so called labourers squatted and it was teeta kehan....cheeeh cheeh..... But if not me then who, if not me then who ....

He was a bad bunny, a bad one at that didn't like to touch Sunny , rather would have soaked the sun , just for fun , always had an erect gun, sing something bitch, sing for me , something , I am the cartel. I supply poppy all over floppy , doppie , noppie, what the fuck,rather , slick , oh father would be pissed , time to apologize.....

He had these iron teeth breaking off a barrier that crossed the mind like a ninja . Post would wear those white trousers, white ganjee with a white towel to shake off sweat . The only thing he wanted was a snow white kingdom. No black , no coal, no fucking slaves motherfucker , that's what we are born for - to be kings , kingdom for whites, motherfuckers , no place to be black ...Yeah I could help them to be garbage , build a garbage damp for them . That's what I am made for , Post , Post for whites ....hohaah.....hoohah .... Post for whites ......hoohah ...hoohah......

Sitting on a chair that was made up of knives of steel , Em , wasn't ready to burn his fingers yet in the neighborhood.

" Enough of your mingling "

" Don't you find friends amidst your color"

Em usually kept quiet in these conversations and kept playing with the soccer ball.

" Be mindful of the hood . Blacks aren't your friends. They don't show their real color. They are meant to live in the forest".

" Mom! Please" Em couldn't shut up for long.

Mom rolled the eyes and went to the dinner table to arrange dinner.

Em did what he did . Em knew what he did . He wasn't Gandhi , he wasn't Mandela , he wasn't Lincoln - then who the fucking who .....

The theatre's been here

With its masks and lies

Lies that protect human

Truth that deceives war

Thorns that wake a man

No side chosen

No color woven

What do you do

Work for wonders

Or work for the self.....

A symbol was being used , kind of a postal stamp to denote Isha's presence . Isha had a vibrating saucer in her hand of which the guests could eat whatever they wanted . Raamdeo wished for chilly chicken - walah! There it was . Mukesh wished for batata wada with authentic chilli and sauce - vodoo- there it was. Motilal wished for his favourite blueberry shake and whoosh- it was served. Everyone was feasting like they never had such a night before. The table was small and the guests were large in number. Mukesh and Motilal were elbowing each other to get space and better view of Isha who stood still with an incredulous smile. Saliva rolled down the edges of the lips and Raamdeo was so hungry that he chewed the entire chicken plate in one gulp with bones being stuck in the throat but he wasn't coughing . He didn't want to disturb Isha . He wanted more . Everybody wanted more . The more they ate, the more dishes arrived out of the shivering saucer and the hungrier they became . What could be said about the kofley house beside the koughing house beside the koughing river where the eagles koughed in hush hush.... The only sounds that echoed in the green valley were the munching sounds of the guests.

Got to ride again the wave, yes the wave I am talking about... But when did you learn to swim. That's a metaphor stupid. Shahid looks out to the depth of traffic . All honking , all poking , all joking.....but you gotta be serious in life .... That's the way to get rewards and awards.....is that monetary? That reward award thing... I am being philosophical stupid. Nearby arose the sea with a light fire , around was a miracle .... Are you laughing? No..... That could be a miracle really..... Sad wasn't Carol, sad wasn't Christmas 🎄, but snow's falling and isn't it exciting with all the hustle of the traffic and smoke right into your mouth...... Ohhho hooo cough cough..... Give me piriton cs dude.... What's that ..... Dexametraphone....or something like that... I work in the pharmacy... At least I work .... What do you do...do do do..... Ru ru ru......sad wasn't Dickens, he after all offered you chickens🐔🍗, George Orwell is holding a protest right at the centre , not left not right , right at the centre..... Ho ho ho..... Do do do....ro ro ru.......

Frequent was the training

Raining all day raining

Chain the arena
None should be out
A necklace to flout
A voice to pout
Riches in doubt
Oh my rich brother
I will dance at your wedding
For the world to see
For the world to woo
Who cares about the Poor's flu
We got the wealthy shoe
We got the queen's necklace's brew.....
Oh mother
You are the goddess
Hope you make me one too
For I too
Wonder about the fair skin too
No one got a clue
No one' s got a clue.,..

The books were lying idle, as idle as me , lost in thoughts, maybe, maybe is a strong thing if you have the patience to listen, for maybe is not bound, maybe is not sure, maybe is not sure of the future . It gives you a tip or two about the present, maybe you are right , maybe you are wrong ,who knows , maybe doesn't know nor do I , maybe......

Pondering over a thick rush of blood

What doesn't come out

Whatever that goes in

Intimated by debate

Slow thinker of a rebate

Anchor of a cheap bait

How do you cling on

How do you let through.....

A newspaper was smelling garlic, someone chopped along with a finger, Halloween for a singer, how many days to linger , rolling was a hot dish, cried hard the fried fish , switch to a chocolate Swiss, how short is your dress miss......say cheese Isha say cheese.....

I slept in a bed, the bed had death written all over it, spikes and likes all over, signals of circling life, mind wanted to check out, a child wanted to be a star, who would go that far, who would say

How would you feel......

Mr Saavy was on his feet when the call came from Shahid and he wanted to chat for long. Shahid wanted to give his cigarette holder to Sara so she could trade it for a higher price. War makes you do things . Buy cheap sell dear.... Dear to dear ones .... Cheap from dear ones

.... Sara was in a flux about the whole bedlam issue and Mr Makata would have praised her beauty amidst the chaos but he chose to remain silent for he thought " Mr Makata is not that smart to praise a beauty"

" What you doing here feeding on our incomes" Sara would all day nag her sister like an old lady . She always wanted to be the boss of the house. See after all that's not her fault after all she made living by serving other drinkers and she was a drinker herself after all and once again not needed after all better haul paul....paul bogan how much promotion did you provide for your videos .... Is it such a life recording videos and blogs day in day out and then paying people to watch them .... Whoa .... People need them ...itz called entertainment..... Shloka disagrees .... Madhu kapur wouldn't have raised such difficult daughters in difficult times..... Mr beast flying beast ....what a life ..... Charlie Munger would have bit his upper lip and Warren would have rather traded derivatives....what a life .....Sara's found the love of her life, Ria Badi the famous gossip reporter famously reported ..... Remember the watch I gave you on your birthday that was worth 100 dollars .... What are you joking?. I wore it to the Ipl match and got teased by Pahariya.... Janvi would kill me for that .... Mr Makata is not that smart to recognize pahariya people from the rural and urban ones . Mr Makata doesn't know how to read or write...... what's a soiree .... A party perhaps hosted by Katrina Ivanovna.... Really does she do her dishes or is Mr N Chandra helping her with the eco thing .... That eco wash dishwasher where hands and coal is required ..... Coal is bad for the environment....but only if you burn it not if you wash it and Vicky found some rashes of coal on the dishes .... Cheee....cheeee....bring me cheese. Alia's mother makes some delicious ones .... Oh that rock star's wife .....hmmm..... Got the point......

Set that out in life, that sail that fail that mail, real sense of the lie that came out of the theatres , wonderful was the publicity in a city , a good man with imperfections, companies the accomplishment, an alliance of the truth, is that what Isha meant or was it forgery, no love but such capitalistic sense....Shahid was trying really hard to concentrate hard on the tales of huckleberry finn and then Ernest came up with an old man and his fishing trips. Was he so unlucky that he got no fish and the young boy came by his side to console or was the console on the hand of the gamer playing Fifa . Was it that hard to get a fish or was it slippery , ask the damn gamer.....

Worst of all distractions

A thought became one of the imagination

Reluctant being good thing

Thing is being bling

Broke in a heated fing

Jaw dropping chicken wing

Imagination of li ning

How many have you killed so far

So far too far

She was cooking the tar

Talking in a bar

Kaleidoscope of a star

A dreamer probably too loud she was. She used to roam in the streets with her track suits on and dreaming of being in the army vehicles roaming the hills of northeast. The golgappa walah near Kanoi college in Dibrugarh was busy sweating and distributing pani puris with his sweat making the puris more delicious. Tina was nineteen and probably too young to be disgusted with such kind of food. But in reality she was unlike all the youngsters making beeline at the golgappa counter. She was waiting for her boyfriend Harsh to arrive and go for a short walk to grab a plate of momos . He seemed too excited to run his bike and was restless. As soon as he reached near,"I cleared it "

"What are you talking about"

"I cleared our dream CDS yaar"

Tina was a bit shocked on hearing the news. She too had given the exam and had no information about results being declared that day . Harsh was talking about her dream exam and he already nailed it. She immediately took her phone out and checked her number. She was not on the list.

It takes sometimes years for a relationship to build and a second to break . It was similar in the case of Tina and Harsh . The School lovers broke then and there . No more dates . No more looking back. It's been 5 years . Harsh had already joined the army as a lieutenant and Tina was still looking for a job. The news had already come in that alqaeda leader zawahiri had been drone shot while he was in his balcony . It kind of confused Tina . Was she happy or sad or it really didn't matter. Scratching her nail paint off her leg thumb she began wondering about her life and dreams . One of her college farewell shirts had a memento written on her sleeve " hope you become an army officer" . Those dreams and wishes were vanishing slowly with real life turbulence on the surface. Hopes are like tight rope walking stunts where once you lose the balance you get grounded.

The greens were lot greener in the monsoons of those Burmese jungles . Tina wondered how and what would life reveal after she joined Hulfa while trekking through those jungles. ' Here the wise and dead come to life ' one of the guides in the militant outfit echoed in her ears. As soon as she reached the camp she was astonished to see a bonfire being lighted by a person with round spectacles . " You are lucky . Bose is here. Let me introduce you to him." Tina was afraid to approach. Didn't he die in a plane crash just before independence and how young does he look.

" The jungle takes care of your skin and don't you know how the honest rebels become ageless"

Bose was standing erect with a stick in his hand …

" Hulfa has waited long for you"

Why did he say so ? Was she being tracked ? Are destinies already known. Some say everyone has a unique destination . Whether he or she finds out it in time is a riddle in itself. Was Sita's abduction by the mighty Ravana a fantasy or hard reality. Did Rama know too well that Sita could well break that lakshman rekha until he goes in and fights him in Lanka for history to know him and then worship him . Was it all written earlier and Valmiki only interpreted through the Gods.

" Are Gods extraterrestrial?" , Bose asked from the back .

Tina again was scared to hear him . His voice was soft as if someone much younger than her.

"That's what we have been taught" , she made a bold move to answer him.

People in hometown of Tina wondered what she was doing . The eternal beauty who was destined to be a 'granter of wishes' to anyone who kissed her with her heart in it. She joining a rebel outfit was a shocking news to everyone. Her father who was a farmer with epileptic fits harbored so many dreams for her. He was shattered. The road to her home was still muddy and when it rained everyone had to walk barefoot . It was impossible for cars to enter. Godi had promised about the promised land but the promised land multiplied the wealth of Madanis of the world not of Pooran , the farmer and father of Tina . His debt grew multifold but not his harbored dreams . They had shrieked . What dreams the common man dreamt under Godi. Except the rupee weakening against the dollar and his display of power and the might of his rallies nothing had changed . One Muslim friend of Tina had commented that 'feku Godi feks and andh bhakts of his lapets'. Pooja , Tina's child hood friend who lost her husband to alcohol had nothing in the world except her one year old son and two pigs who she hoped would if survived the virus could be sold at a decent price.

"What the politicians say , what they really do and in truth what they really are " looking at the mountains Bose was in deep thought and kind of mumbling to Tina.

" Nothing's changed out there and nothing's gonna change " , for the first time Tina kind of felt free to converse with Bose.

" That's why we are here . To bring change. To change everyone's destiny. And never has been it about only peace. Nothing's greater than generosity and kindness," Bose seemed dreamy . No one in this world or the other could teach Tina about kindness and Bose already knew that.

" We are gonna build nations out of freedom . That's the generous goal now"

" But what about a united India" , Tina was perplexed.

"Are we really free? "

"Are we really free? "

I have been reading about haloalkanes

Good for you

Also haloarenes

Hmmhmm

Halogens attached to alkanes are haloalkanes

So ...

Halogens attached to arenes are haloarenes

Wtf

Plants excrete from the stomata present in their leaves

Momata

Stomata....

Oh yeah stomata....

And miss you...

And I could never remember the periodic table

I would prefer a fable

Periodic table's better

Gud for you

Hmm

All the best

For what

Whatever....

People say many things

Many things weird

Some things stupid

Mostly not of love

Mostly of hate

People's eyes say many things

They see the tree as I can't

They see love as I don't

They care as I can't

They teach as I haven't been taught

People and people

Look inside my heart

Take things for granted

They light the smoke within

They turn the pages of history

As if a burnt kid' s story

They philosophize as no philosopher can't

People and people ....

People and people ....

An inspector you are , are you happy? Oh! that's a wild question, who do you ask , I mean , why do you ask ? Sabotaging the prestige, perhaps, perhaps he couldn't speak , who? That early guy who was late into the night guy and early Into the 30's guy , calm him down , they are the ignorable kind , know nothing kind , buddhu and burbak kind , heh heh ....pichak thu kind ....heh heh.....

Unaware was the unstained , unstained kind he thought in fact later Avni apologized for her statements, everything had to do with everything or something with everything, a kind of blur and confusing statement , she thought , she thought in myriad ways , undedicated perhaps , perhaps uncommon to the natural.

Quantity of 1 litre expressed in metre or in fitter better litter , litter the Dutch nation and see the shock on their faces , the whole world of the West Indies , mind the overthrown donkeys flying around the commonwealth games , honor of the commission- 2.5%, 5%,8%, how much more , spices produced and pasted onto the asses of the Europeans , indeed the globe was there to see, see the quantity joint stock exchanges, Nadia, it's all about the stock's rise , a to and fro and then long term aspect play of the supply and demand scenario, no odd success of the venture. How many followers Sachin , how many subscribers, one quarter of the century, centuries of century, that's too low a square, but how you add to the century part cementing Nadia's place onto the artillery master's crucial difference in a naked battlefield.

Tenth Street was the lane ,the place was bane and profane , Atul was doing his best to reflect light in a situation that demanded attention. 22.0586°N latitude stretching till 22.0697°N latitude.

" My watch isn't that smart anymore " , Atul didn't leave the blackest of situations to joke. Alyssa wasn't one bit amused. All the investigations about the place were kept in safe lockers not revealing the awkwardness of the place absorbing all the light in the world . Atul naturally had a tendency to work slowly and slowly he did. One bit of electron , one bit of wave , one bit of particle , Atul was the only person in the whole lot of avatars to dissect with his bare hands the wave particle duality of the light.

" Ratan wouldn't be too happy with the situation"

" Leave Ratan to his dogs and his charities. This shit is swallowing light like a hungry shark and it wouldn't be long before the whole galaxy disappears just like that"

Alyssa had that look as if she wanted to lock that moment where Atul talked and she listened, Atul worked and she just watched....

Work did prevent her, from all things unnecessary, pity on new words , titty in the newer world , looming heavy was the bell, a pile of building fell, she spoke to her to tell, an illness to sell , lot of nights to dwell , looming heavy was the bell....

Rising was the embrace , deep expressions of a lace , pleasure seeking brother, a hair loose character, hands too cold rather, couldn't catch that ball, it went too high, out of exosphere crusty little sphere , noiseless Bounderby dear , facts facts facts mere , facts facts facts dear.....

Information was scarce, grave was the speech, graver were the words, Nikhil Kamath didn't write those but just came out instantaneously.

He spoke of the economy, politics, Gandhi, Nehru and wrapped up with the slogan "Jai Bhim".

"Drop it" his mind said

"Jai Bhim"

"Don't speaketh with plaineth, people would come to know sooner rather than later that you are Ajaat"

"Jai Bhim"

Bhagat wouldn't like it. He doesn't want this movement to be caste based again. The same caste based politics all over again.

"Jai Bhim" this time the roar was louder.

"Bose is watching you. Better be in attention"

"Jai Bhim" , Nikhil shouted so loud that he fell off the stage almost unconscious.

"Accountability is the factor – square means square and a circle means round, you can't stand for long on the tip of the triangle especially with a wind speed of 20-25 at that range."

"Tejas N73N°is made for that sir.

Faster it is, lighter it is, better it is.

It can pierce through mountains with the s mode and can dive underwater with n mode ."

"What about time?"

There was silence in the room.

The room had an off beat green color, not too green, not too blue, turquoise might be, but was a color that soothed the eyes. There were the flags that cried devotion, passion and service. Country first.

India first, was the silence that echoed through the hall.

Anand looked at his watch that was as basic that a pilot's watch could be and he was getting late.

"It's the pilot sir"

There was a question again in the silence of the Colonel.

"It's not the Tejas but who's flying it. There's only one person in the whole world, past or present who could do that and that's Chandragupt's secret love Isha"

Anand was feeling restless.

"The Mauryan empire stood not only on the expertise of Kautilya but the ultimate trained warriors under the arms of Chanakya, Isha. Guerrilla combat, arms, hand to hand, martial art, swords, you name it. Isha had the dexterity only a soldier could dream about."

"There are stories of Isha leaving the empire in the later years of the Mauryan Empire. Some say she flew to the other side of the galaxy, some say she preferred the black sea, but Major Anand here believes he could find her in the jungles of Amazon."

Anand immediately stood up without breathing.

"Major Anand, have you traced her."

"Search is on sir"

"Any specifics"

"Sorry to say sir but I cannot reveal"

The Colonel wasn't a bit impressed.

"You know the gravity of our situation"

"Sir! Yes sir!"

"Then where's Isha"

"That cannot be revealed, sir!"

"Okay, enough. Can you bring her in our camp"

"कोशिश जारी है सर"

"कोशिश...fucking कोशिश।"

We are short on time Major"

"Sir! Right sir!"

"Dismissed!"

Huen Toany sang the dang, fang was in the gang, a fan he carried, lan was discovered by him totally, brutally, totally, frooti was drunk in those tyring times by his companion Dingsingpha. Sumungpha grew wild seeing his.

"She has these tits , that fits into bits what say dids."

Sukapha grew worried that Huen Toang and Sumungpha could get into war of swords, words, lords, gords, Oh godzilla....

"It's like I am sitting on lava, seeing them smile at each other."

Dingsingpha was constantly writing and the whole Ahom dynasty scrambled to get O2 for she had to while so many & the trees had to fall too many deny, Finding Fanny! Where Goa! Good lord Fuck the Portugese...

Anonymous -> Have you heard of Chipko

Isha -> You yourself are one

Anonymous -> I mean the Chipko movement

Isha -> Yes, I read somewhere

Anonymous -> Guwahati is having one of it's Chipko moments

Isha -> It was about saving trees na

Anonymous -> Yes... Yes... They are trying to build a flyover by cutting old trees. Students and citizens have been protesting day & night.

Isha: You could see what's happening with Global warming.

Anonymous -> Oil & drilling stuff

Isha -> what?

Anonymous -> I mean to be carbon neutral

Isha -> That we are

Anonymous -> So, you are neutral in love too... what about the heart, is that neutral too?

Isha -> Shut up ...

The old judge had happened to recognize Rohit albeit in a peculiar way, bound to eat, as shown on the glancing terrace, on one side was the rich and young Ananya, whom he thought was quite sexy, in particular, fitting in a tailor shop, wow! She could be the one, what was her name again, Ananya, form of the disappearing, Narendra wanted to finish the sentence in Naini prison while conversing with Sardar Vallabhai Patel, discourses of the

Queen's policies and the hatch back, get to the box earlier hurrying along the stupefors of time, a half baked lime, Rohit thought, even furs on the street, please repeat.

Ananya asked, a footman arched and backed, slight ripple on the stars, make me a mouth that arches over a dome, grey and an L march just like Narendra wanted for the uniformed soldiers, thick muffled bars over the chest Mars, ok! You planning a trip Elon, who was with, then, Isha would relish for a moment, support the nation, or place your heart in place of the nation, that you can't or feel helpless or feel the emotions of deprived, an unwanted feeling, but Narendra and Rohit wanted to pay a tribute to time, singing praises of Anne's diary, where was it lost, perhaps Subhash had marched till the end of time where Hindustan held its ground despite all...

The party hall was full of noise, chatter and clatter all over the breaking of Mahatma's fast. Quiet but to only himself, Amit had kept the fast unto death along with Gandhi, but no one knew, except Shreyas. "These memories would serve me better in times to come!" Shreyas would remind Amit. Outside the drawing room was a motif that recovered their senses of British rule, wandering like Karan, sometimes into the past, sometimes into the future > "quit it", Karan, don't overdo it", Karan was sweating it. Out all on the Yandaboo treaty and helping in a way the Assamese out of the Burmese lands, 'the black days may be over,' Manor দিন cannot repeat", Karan wearingly said.

Something humorous, off course, off the course in the menu, coming in the way of the blind, a blind path fold coming in the way of the blinds, Virat to showcase his motoring skills. Zendya was impressed, she wanted to be by the shop window and shop for a curious pattern, partly for a flirt, and an oppression for opposition, why not, all in a circle, love of Zendya and Virat, dancing the tap dance, tap, tap, tap, tap, Oh! I want a tap dance and Zendya obliged.

Utterly disorderly their accumulation of thirty black shoes racked and stacked up in extremely hot condition, Virat got to pick and choose beside the shop window and Zendya but his mind was in getting Rama up and running, back from nirvana, back from his pose of meditation, back to the third eye occult. Virat had a responsibility & he knew it too well...

An old man came from the back, reversing the cycle of looking back, back from what? Did it shock people, Virat asked, he was concerned more about Iltumush's secret intent, was he again building an army, Virat had the weapon of choice though, that weapon to reveal for later stages, now he had Raskolnikov up for breakfast , for the sufferings were huge and Raskolnikov almost dropped dead and then again alive ....like the watchmaker Karan again turning the wheels of time.....

Kamseen was eighteen about her age, an adage about age. No brain was too selfish for the hundreds of moves that passed through the spectrum. Isha loved it hotly and totally, mutual leaf on to the trees, mufatlal, muft ka hulfat, unselfish was the shooting in Tuberville, manners of a barber's block, round the clock, instead was consciousness, streets busy with themselves, extravagant for Rohit to measure the liking, wanna go hiking, nothing for the viking. The collection fell too quickly over the stairs, look back at ten O' Nadia, speaking to the outlaid table, sable, dabble in stocks then, dalaal street is waiting to dive, temper of Virat went soaring to the lights of the bitter happenings, spiraling was the shape, do you want a grape O' Nicki, show me your ass then, cuddle to the sitting down sofa, wrist was never the same, lame was the exquisite joy, such a ploy, such a coy, boy, sun had It's mastics painted on the wall, looking directly at the eyes, Isha shies, summer after summer, waiting under the tree, that bitch. She came and waited for her turn to get hitched, impressions of young people, O' did you edit young India, fashion dresses going out of fashion, for no reason whatsoever, sight of a pump with a dhai kilo ka haath, one thing led to another, and bitches were fighting on top of one another, & then the chutzpa

Siren... fuck...

Cloud on sudden shrill, march the shrill then, what about a religion abroad, go abroad and fuck the migas where they belong, humorously of course, heh heh heh intercourse with Mrs. Daway, Shreyas was following a curious pattern, piping all through the Queen's necklace, are you talking about Mumbai, hai hai Bombay meri jaan , motor car was passing by the red district & then the thought of God just passing through the techniques & the days passing through the same thing again & again, the bitch that kissed that latrine black brush all the way down

No it wasn't love, it can't be love, such irritation, such darkness, & such indecency,

But the banana nation has to face it alone

After all face for it all & on the black

Blue and the hue & she's got the clue,

Is it lost on her, fainter & painter,

Untitled she wants, she wants to control Kamathipura where the profound faith was taking her to any talent that was specially designed or established in the moulds of Paris La Curec. La Chirac wanted to inaugurate, but Sara rejected, saying she was too beautiful to be pictured in a frame, damn she was an onlooker towards the miracle of the inevitable exclamation, positioned to make the straw retire, whose mess you talking about, carrying the outstretched hand, on the distant pose of the bandstand lodging to get shaved like Ulysses man....

A sound echoed through the door and Isha went through the vigor, was it a beginning or an end maybe a pocket knife in the hands of Mukesh and he was staring at the sofas, stare Mukesh, stare better, better for later then, the leaves were staring at nowhere, I look like a bhikhu asking for alms then, what you want in absence through all the ages, all through the ages, voice of the Gods spoke through them, and she wanted to marry a God nursing her way through. Oh! Sally what you doing in influencing her through the oddest of things , what you want in human, in that personal touch , uff, uff bhai hai, lai eat the lai , then shift and clean , badshah bhai told swift was swifter than the so called Rolls Royce , do you agree Isha , I ain't talking to you coz you are more interested in markets, maybe a sort of pleasure, or is it pressure, sell in self , believe in self direction onto one direction, touching the thinkers of no direction, a pleasure getter of sorts......

Give me the way back

For suppositions aren't superstitions.

Judging by the way you look

I ain't going back

Back to where I belong

Are those cats & rats

The dogs with the fats

They ain't hiding

Why you wanna hide me

In the Heights of wuthering

Where the English before the mutiny rose

To the cries of Sati's pose

Days have gone by

Years have breezed by

Was it do or die

Why did Bhagat die

Innocent, young without a lie

Where was do or die

All must be an exaggeration

Politics, youth and nation

Honey, fame & fashion

Better to talk about passion

Better to take a piano lesson

Give me the way back

For suppositions aren't superstitions....

There were orders from Paresh and Subhash didn't like them, unity at borders at all cost, hard to see through, no visitors allowed, Tina wanted to get in, get in a look of Paresh and Subhash together, how have you been? Is Karan still on the run or they caught hold of him,

What was the situation in Kalimpong, is the judge Sai still free, Tina also wanted to know the whereabouts of Aurangzeb. It wasn't without any motive that Aurangzeb had destroyed so many temples, the present day is all for to see, but what about the future, Karan was working on that. The night scene of the statue of Liberty with a music of incredible suspense, chaos and commotion in the midst of serenity, Karan was hanging on the side arm of the Liberty statue to find the time zone of Aurangzeb's death, 1707. The unlucky part for Karan was that the material exclusion of Aurangzeb from the material world was before Ramanujan's number, 1729, otherwise history would have been different & likewise the present & the future.

Primitive were the legs, primitives were the men, still found the right way towards the bay, which way, which way, gay smile rather, lenses on the ground, though some flew and some blew their chances, Nadia dances, bucket load of sand and sticks onto the skin, red stones flared up, teams were nonchalant, reviewing all of their chances, Nadia dances, sitting in the front seat, gasping breath for the Nanny as Leo took her in his arms, that left Nadia in tears, still Nadia dances, what you doing with the slave skull unearthed by archeologists, dreary manner, tooth poking on the wolves, a wolf pack, bars of tea drinkers, recovered his senses, Anand, looked around the jungle, no one, literally, no one, still, Nadia dances.....

Hanged in generosity, is she, from an alleged conspiracy, there to her clients, present at nothing, nothing at all, leading to arising death, presence of good enough listeners, Isha, are you listening, or trying out jewelry & make up, distaste of law, that is, income was bread and butter dipped in mayonnaise, leave it at that, Mayweather, otherwise the boxing cubs would rise at a reasonable pace, Sondesh, give Isha some sondesh, not for the army, damn! Started as a relative, invested heavily in dark stores, 1 second delivery, oh! Negative minutes delivery, you thought of it, in fact the delivery arrived before you thought, lunch arrived before you starved, battle won before you fought.

Decorated were the stands and settled were the bands, friends don't get into a settled mode for Post didn't want to get rid of the shame he had through the downturn. Post had bought all the put options available on 25th Feb on the Tesla stock but Musk out of just nowhere appeared on the screen supporting Trump and plus what, Kamala slipped.

Tesla's stock was making new highs and Post was on the wrong foot.

Selling lies, going away flies, I got no time wasting, go away lies, Wiz and Bhim however shies...

Black has a new beginning that too with a tattoo, lick my white ass motherfuckers...

It was in the subconscious mind or the inner consciousness, Mathews was a bit puzzled. He was perplexed and puzzled about aiming his shotgun. It was double barreled or what he didn't know.

He was naive at that. He was confused whether he was stationed there to shoot a Jew or an Arab. Who did Palestine belong to. He had no answer to the three religions: Judaism, Christianity, and Islam. Was the United Nations vote counted. When the Britishers left Palestine under who's guard was all left for, Mathews thought all holding that arm but inside was crying for his home farm. An Arab bystander spat phlegm on a Jew passerby and the Jew walker innocently crossed by. What degradation! What humiliation! For the Holy land! God would cry! Angels would cry! Even Mathews cried...

What would you do for a land

Arms and bombs to defend

Alone, you can't withstand

The force of such holy land

How dare you offend

How dare you step on that sand

It's our holy land

No voice would be allowed

To speak against the lord
No land would be spared
To act against God
He is the almighty
Bow your heads
Be his slave
For He is the only one brave

What kind of legacy do you look for? To be the known or the unknown. Fighting the wrong, writing about it in a song and all that, what after that? What happens next? Who gives a damn about a song? The same way an independent candidate falls among the heavyweights in elections. But you can't predict that.

You can't predict the wave. Best you could share and stand in queue on the election day! Is education necessary to be enlisted as a candidate? Shahid thought. He himself read, studying and learning how could academic degrees define the eligibility and ability of any candidate in a democracy, Shahid shouted. And shouted at the inequality, illiteracy, radicalism, unemployment and sufferings that he saw doorstep to doorstep. He shouted because he was angry at not being given the permission to smoke weed. It's the holy grass, he argued and smoked whatever was leftover. That night eight goons came over and picked him straight to the rehab. That's all for smoking, that's all for shouting, that's all for protesting, that's all for freedom in a so called democratic nation. That's all...

That's all...

The schoolwork was all overloaded with heavy' duties on the science work and the social work and the environmental work and of course Macbeth . Who remembers those lines as if Christiano was paying some fines of previous birth. He was for better at dribbling the ball but the English master took no notice of that. Rap that! Rap that Sonnet you idiot if you can. Look at Wayne, he is doing so well. Christiano spilled the beans on the floor at lunch time and the ayah was furious but she swept. And listening to Wayne's verses she wept. Mahalanobis was busy making five fear plans inspired from Europe's history and architecture and technology and the fish wala laughed at that. Where would the fishes go when your hydropower plants are built. They would go to your nets you idiot.

There's no George Orwell to save them. Breed them and kill them. That's the rule you fool. Elections are approaching and better auction the election ballots to that company who has bribed more and make sure the election commission gets a bounty. Yeah they are fair. Elections are as fair as the spread of communalism and as fair as the killing of a girl child. It's a birth right. Now better sell that branded hair-oil. Lots of dandruff. To erase and cost capitalism to cease. Fees! Fees! Don't forget the taxes, the GSTs. Though they go to the pockets of the tax officers, and the capitalists...

The throat was desperate for a smoke and it kind of irritated Manoj. He had no cigarette on him. There was a bystander smoking a beedi and he asked him for a puff. It had no stuff, no green stuff, no holy stuff, no cannabis stuff on it. But he smoked and made circles in the air. Manoj used to live in an one room apartment and last year on Diwali, painted it pink with Asian paints.

Since then the stock of Asian paints had moved up 30% and on the other hand his own savings were down 50% and he was desperate for a new job. He used to make flutes, though he didn't himself play the made excellent ones but the business wasn't that good. He was listening to Elvis's 'blue suede shoes' and was in jubilant mood. He had a passion for shoes and immediately made up his mind that he would craft hand made leather shoes custom made. When his family got a whisper of that they went crazy. They went wild for they considered shoe making was a trade for the lower caste. Fast! Fast! Better fast! On the full moon day otherwise you would be an outcast, his family members warned.

If he could he would *shoot* his own ones but he went back and made the flute.

A framed photograph was hanging on the wall. Lionel couldn't figure out whether the photograph was of an actual live starry night or was it a photograph of an artwork. It looked so dreamy. He had seen many real life starry nights before, once in the desert, once in the hills and always in his hometown. He had noticed that as his childhoods the stars weren't that brightly visible nowadays. Probably they had become shy, he thought. Lionel's mother was shouting in the kitchen about the pills he forgot to consume before dinner. He forgot the count of no. of medicines the times and the number of medicines he had to consume in a day. What disease do I have?

Lionel often wondered in his regular visits to the psychiatrist.

After all he did was write sonnets and poems all day and night. Was it a crime he thought? When will you earn? When would you get a regular job? Regular complaint of the family.

But he knew nothing of the materialistic business. He knew rhymes, emotion, love, misery, and pain, and he wrote all about it. But who gives a damn!

Lionel did. He swallowed a pill and sat down to write about the photograph, about the artwork, about the starry night.

"Why don't you need a passport?" asked Jamila: "I travel on the magical carpet and it's so swift that it passes the borders without a glitch.", said Luis. "Anyways you are an Arunachali and you don't need a passport or visa to travel to China."

Jamila was trying to politicize the issue. I don't want to delve on that as a matter of fact. Anyways, China's not a democracy," Luis said, and then flew on his carpet. All of a sudden the carpet bent space & time and landed him in a Mughal court.

He was bedazzled to see the architecture, the interior carvings and the lonely peacock throne. Luis approached a lonely girl in the sand and she said that her name was Selena. She had been bought far away from Spain and was a court singer. Though she sang in Spanish the Mughals appreciated and liked it.

In the meantime a crowd gathered for the assembly, courtly meeting and seeing Luis and his magical carpet the soldiers immediately surrounded him and put him in chains. Aurangzeb was so happy he rewarded golden coins on his troops and ordered the magical carpet to be presented to him.

Read the letters wired down the fence, the backyard had a puppy's tail wagging downwards, summer came to us though, something in the collared pitch that Isha recognized, hey sitting down (a puppy), bark, bark at the reader older than eight, reading since six, better looking in school dress, funnier the names, a foot longer in jerking, jerk the dork, folks call me a struggler, every summer in a picture and reading graphic novels, Sayanika was twenty times more beautiful than you could ever imagine, the imagination was a court house good in good reads, good in a goody, good in a fool house, spending tokens in a Mississippi Counter, any pictures of a photographer, take her down the memory lane, eye him with a curiosity....

Snow white wearing linen, Coal Black in suede, hospitality was habitual, the senior tower over the central tower, one pulled out of the dust, a habitual offender in Kamathipura, salt for the cows & goats, sounds better, stuck in a leaf pudding, darkened eyes made the laughter more sudden.

The father had nothing to say, his blue eyes lightened up the happiness, and Nadia was at the fore front of the 'Mrityu bahini'. Summer passed, winter passed, nothing happened. Trees were running their dramas, a medium sized character, did you mind the drama of the giants, acceptable could be the victory...

As anyone might say, stories are stories, and facts are facts, the great wall of China in a fact but the Parakind wall was said to be an unheard story, though still we heard of it. Maybe a Bard in his deathbed told us about it. Lived over an age ranging for 5000 years and fears no force could ever overpower it. The wind told stories of the walls ironically attacking whoever and whatever came within 30 meters around. The lines were green and nostalgic wear off in between. However, a virgin lady Ash lived within it's promises, no one had ever seen, no one had ever touched. A taboo about the untouchable lot, but she was the only one within. Trees, fruits, ferns within the walls spoke to her and she to them and no one else... 20, her age, never increasing, never dreaming...never decreasing.....

Karan wanted to be found, go mad at real things not the stupid rings, guilty was the tongue, marked down 2nd time, the flames and the lone room were talking to oneself, an organ left to cry, no reason for unbaked excitement. The time was killed for Gandhi and Nadia knew it too well , a worse thing to write, a gold spot to drink, a gold spot to write; Shakespeare came in late with his drunk wife Isha, who was eating porridge & laughing, the happy tears also had a dream, saw the visions together, moving about the end of the room, lap full of moments, advanced to eagerness, the clock sounded like glass, alas, at last....

Passed by the hard working fellow

A sobriety to swallow

Drumming was the hot window
Accumulated the enquiries
Curious pattern of motor cars
Passing by the blinks
An overcoat that clinks
Rumored street that thinks
Armor off the chinks
Apologize to the male hand
These are pre historic times
All about the male ego
There we go Beezo
Hey hard working fellow…
A sobriety to swallow…..

Suddenly a loud thud, just that thud, loud but thud just from behind, all was dark and a woody dark night where you wouldn't wanna be. Ria was in a dark palace just about waiting for her husband to arrive and that was an attempt of her to be secure. As she had contemplated with her darkest of thoughts, would she escape the maze or fall further into it,

An attempt at a fling, a lands on experience or what else…

Why not kill her, then, then and there, in all credulity, in all dearness, in all eternity, bear the shame of own mother, darn mother, you call her, isn't the cause of all the trouble – Ash was thinking as if aloud, as if talking to herself.

Off studies, oh! That really kicked off and then stopped, stopped & stopped. Nat could have persuaded her to pursue, maybe economics, maybe micks or the mimics of sort and the possibilities were immense, but Nat didn't want that, she didn't want Ash to go that far...

All singing and praying, a gallop of the horse and all stood silent, like the river on a full moon night. Do you mind him laughing at that, now, 'just now'. Isha would be glad to help, her whips ready for the slips, sudden and frightful, as if in a rage, as if a sage in a cage. The stone-head was circumstantial, picked up from the crowd showcased into a crowd funding of sorts, a break of heart shouted again, eating all her mashvik, preparing the brute in mates to fill in the big carts singing again and praising, get the hell out of here, blasphemy and all looked all around for attention and then the memory walked still like a glass fill, twenty yards down the town, make yourself comfortable, at the table beside the stable, be able and proud table twenty roubles then for all that and that .....

Perhaps an embrace, Isha wished, wishes and all that was heard by the world, that worked around with expenses, wanted to arrange a salary, readily, freddidy, fiddily, silly, perhaps an acquaintance of sorts, excitement in part.

Isha: Is the ceremony over?

Mahi: Write anything you like.

Isha: Is it over?

Mahi: What?

Isha: The ceremony.

Mahi: Write that down.

Isha: Have you been listening?

Mahi: My ear works fine.

So he believed, Mahi, great hopes and the dopes of the Popes, enthusiasm particularly nothing to do with looks de salon, a press meet where the stars did this jittery – glittery – biliary scene and Isha was happy, OK! Happy, that's an exaggeration, what about the wedding

In for postponed due to you, due

To me, due to an uninstalled loo,

Doo doo doo doo...

Write anything you want, twenty copecks for a page, credit as much money as you want, one day for a joke, credit was heard for sending the pension, Oh! Yes credited that too.

Howz the pen working, hmm, fine like the old lady on the old staircase , possible arrangements, impossible pacts, 'Gandhi and Irwin's pact fool

Irwin came down stairs crying after the part, for the love was too much and the pain too lonely....

The draw was all hopeless, being hopeless could be fun, if you really imagine , Tina wondered how, with all the public justification,

And the defence was not ready, doesn't necessarily mean the damn borders but the lawyer who was pursuing Isha and her regrets, that would be a strong word 'in court 'regrets', nevertheless the desk was moving for under table deals.

Intentional to be ineffective, first impression was that Tina first pleaded not to read, the first lead on the bed, first feed on instead, papers mislaid, how much misinformation, how many losses more, Oh! Better watch out, many more...

Your hoodies aren't goodies to be fuddu and foodies, Isla was blunt in her words and dress, she was wearing a red hue with the narrow tunnel drawing towards her, please give the mic to Baby Jones, for he got a baby to cuddle and Isha's got a candlelight shoot, I need focus damn it, a huge comeback of sorts from the film fraternity with the bass guitarist giving more importance to Swift songs, you like it wh huh wh zuch! Music's gonna change, whether you like it or not, shouted Rushdie, fault of the fake buttocks. The red car trying to drink a bin of gasoline and the men trying to hold that old key, put her in a bag, make her beg, that old hag, he was also chained that Rushdie, mayhem and chaos in the mind but body well positioned, keys on the drawing board, make me free, free me...

I don't care about the odor while here was the other and the door envying the window & the window about the grass. Are we fools, asked the shameless mounting the heavenly sound.

All felt humiliating like a precise union

Of sun, of moon

Of boon, of doon

Have them soon

Believe the lone room...

Nothing beside the burden, a strong bar caring about the fast car so much to talk in a fast walk

The willow made a sound

As if from mid of the sex

Do you call that beauty

Beastly or Vulgar

Own choice

Own rejoice...

A pillow talk for me, Isha, what else do you have in mind while the engine stalls and the car talks like an address changing castle, were you late in the evening Isha with all the hostile bids coming in, bug for a bugger in direction of Inglis the smart headed boy who could be inexcusable with all his debauchery. Isha came late like white snow in the desert and the rolling cameras kept rolling, she had no idea what the veil looked like, what a hailstorm looked like, what a snowfall felt like, holy lamb of God, that's what it's like. He was young and handsome that Inglis of a fellow and knew of a bid of Hinglis with words like loot on my foot, my ring. Ishe rose to say like two pairs on church boringly sang to the already bored God with all the sermons and loud gals singing in empathy, sympathy apathy & therapy... Isha wanted to position herself as a lovely, nice photograph with Inglis still... still... Oh! That could be a story... another line...another time.....

Noisy shoes lapped the thoughtful

Own steps of the wind

Serenity of the voice

Footsteps own choice

Lost to river & stars

Asleep was the mood

Rose again the hood

Whip cracks of the hoof

Plain language aloof

Eyes wandered into the sunroof

Wonderful in a group

Little laugh of the troop...

Did it not somehow come down,

Book spread open to reveal about the

Secrets of Ashni who was the heat of the sun, revealed by Perry that they had survived the heat though. The walkers and the Falkers, the lowers and the lovers sharing a room with multiple authors', abused all night blow by blow, slow to slow at the moment, cold prune of a heart where was Perry making the chocolate Perry Londonberry the cables passing through the luchka puchka of the market and the swing master Ashni weaving a fairy tale with her hand standing atop those cables, consoling to the fables, a little license to dance eh...

Never ever the scene was forgotten where Perry parted for a hundred years, not in it. Having come back, having unknown the little perfect of a Perry, was gone now to the players. The nizam empire was all lost but not the dead souls, "How much for 300", the land shivered when it asked, the whole atmosphere was grail with killed birds and shivering bones.

Left to not, loving the economy eh, building again the Royal army leh, powerful enough to ask a cousin, dead souls on the lead avatar, that's a beautiful one, ain't it.

Such marginalised characters on the whole, asking for a dead soul that was wandering through the Bedlam kingdom in search of the princes. Radhika whose father was a merchant by trade and she was too beautiful.

Prince Pandya couldn't take his eyes off and often his father could have said anything, but did not, for he was an alcoholic , so went about grumbling, swimming on the silly areas, that's completely reckless, on his part, falling in love with Radhika, that's how he shelters life. His personality for instance, and then think what kind of property he had amassed, she couldn't be certain about the number of rooms, let alone her own bedroom, and an inner meaning screamed, it was a pity, looking at the fifty sixty, don't sit on the floor, look at the crescendo, it has a quality, don't ya feel reckless, completely reckless.

Wouldn't life be on the whole, as if extracted from the depths of her words, "No"

It wouldn't, it would perhaps, if you wanted and went through all her essays. Ria was an essay writer, a good one at that, she kept herself busy with characters, she kept revolving and evolving with them, perhaps Ria could write a novel, or polling, or trolling, or short stories, but the thought of the essays were better with live stories, she also watched live fights, one championship where the fighters punched blood into each other's faces, she liked it;

Strange. The table was tumbling as she wrote, and gave a loud shed to it, "Stop it"

Right now, I am thinking, thinking about what the black karate kid or the black snowman you were trying to build with White Snow..... is it possible? Possible are impossible things if you take a step back just to realize. But then you are just imagining things from reality, is it augmented reality, Bima Das shooting the governor, she had to do it. She was in love with Bhagat and those in love with Bhagat would love to shoot any governor, past, future or present. Sitting on the chair, idle, fingers revolving, the pen like kids do with their homework, table turn table and let the words come often, let it be of the India Pakistan match even, how she would have loved to watch it live, then she didn't know the schedules and the desire to travel far away places, but Paris was different. Wanting to be in the arms of her lover....is the want an augmented reality, ain't it? Watching titanic laid back, rusting under the black blankets, or, Notting Hill for that matter, all dreams, huh!

At every step in surprise, though several times awoke Raskolnikov as if out of a slumber to confess about the door of the law, "I am right, I am alright, I murdered Maniram & Piyoli, I am right, I am alright" sweat pouring out of his jaw line. There was no sign of Meg who looked in awe at his perspiration. He caught her several times by the hand to shake himself up from the nightmare but he was well aware not to.

"Let it be, let it be".

She was schooled during the war

And then she understood the meaning

Was there physical pain

Cold water with rain.

She had had enough

But she endured

Flowers that kept stray?

A storm in the room

A roof in the boom

Self love in the gloom...

Fun being scolded, naah! None would agree, but Nat could deliver a lecture onto that, she was the youngest and the wisest, study being given the full recognition along with attention, Charlie wouldn't mind being with Nat, would he.

Really good was the chicken, ain't it Nat, the poor lady was busy firing advice, at least a hasty taste on a race, right up to the face, tie up your lace. Nat was up for a brace, she had once been to Lahore, and had eaten

Gulati kabab, mmm... nice to meet you, pehnji, with a tinge of olfactory noise, duty of Nat to greet her, pehnji+ olfactory factory noise......

Nat wanted to go through the mughal phase when Shah Jahan was building the Red fort oh!! Baba how many bricks it took, how many men employed, all into the statistics book of Joe, are you offended by the thirst of it, let it be all, let the ball play by the hall, fun loving Nat sure about the fall, never understood a word or cared about; was she annoyed about Katherine being a catholic or her mum disagreeing to their nuptial, disturb the modern literature as much as you want and since then it has been a touch of vicissitude, not the will of God, after all, God wills nothing and everything at the same time to be the root of the confusion, complex problems, with calculus and all.

Nat came to Joe's house after the fall, studied by all simplifications, went to the cinema with father, brother or whatever, as if Nat was delighted, as delighted as she was on her marriage; wanted straight face to face, scar of the taste, no satisfaction on the responsibilities, infrequent visits about nothing, nothing on the loose strands, hands on the wrist, chee cheh, the Kalu kaluta is standing on the sewage canal and clearing the pot? did you doubt yourself ever, unhappiness is a thing, patient water with a patient feather.....

Nat went about the hill, along with the blue umbrella. Bond was asking her some questions, she had no idea about, about the whereabouts of Frada and the ring, the ring. Particularly? An interesting thing? Not only for Bond but for the seven kingdoms.

There was a time where lived a tale, ongoing sale for that matter, Nat's chatter for that matter, where lived the big foxes and ones, falling before the snow wall was the weary, fear. The teary, sheary, imagine the jiggling jagglong molecules or rather atoms or rather electrons, for that of Nat's chatter, she wanted to ask the big boys about Boyles law & how P $\propto$ 1/v be even if she preferred the much much, puch puch, kuch kuch over the overloaded syllabus that the fuddu teacher gave- Oh! I am in uniform bcoz I know the uniform civil code, I know history, sociology, I know current affairs, and the affairs of illegal men fuddu chuddu .....

The butterfly flew over the bored and scattered leaves, Oh I am so bored then. Stop writing about me then, and the chamber just opened to reveal that the dead sea wasn't actually dead and Anand lived just beside and under with his 17 men who were saved from the Nazi camps. Their search had not ended and still they were in search of the furher who they believed still lived underground.

Horror into the fold, quarelled the old about Nat's age, she's sweet sixteen, still, escape her eyes then, reports about a campaign, Wazir Alam was on the mood of a cint war, whom you serving then.! The project was new amid all the troubles Hind kush faced, dedication was more towards appreciation of the nation, concerned were the diamond merchants about the safety of the Kohinoor, a beloved instead, pens breaking the flock of high water, heavy water rather for nuclear reactor, cure him in the bed for the bed is sleeping and the royal guard is sleeping and also the queen. Natalie, Nat for short, she used to make shorts earlier, now she has moved on to a longer form of pajamas, value of the vault I suppose.....

Thousands matter in the run of votes and voters did turn out that day, quickly made a plan, God knows whether Isha would be as good as her earlier phase, two different sides, Isha & Natalie, proposed campaign onto the questions, who's question thy ask? Chart facing downwards, crying and all, talking about how the world faces starvation, poverty, war, with what resilience, hanging it on a hunger strike, big mouth shouldn't cry, bitch, what, you complaining about Nat, the old nurse's dirty panty, check check...

The clock was bleeding nine and Nat was raring to go, irony it seems, what has been decided then, to be enthusiastic about the beauty of Nat or grieve over her new found love, won't receive the payments then, you can't inherit bastard, the great Indian bastard who is lonelier than ever, clapping for ever, getting late to the court and rally of constitution and articles, elegant was the blame of Nat, alarming were her steps, wrinkled and dressed like that her suitor went away on a haunted visa, she felt like meaning on the tower of Pisa, talks of fear and war, an entry door on the floor, straight to hell Isha said, are you interested, a civilian past, the middle age puckering up the dress, go away, suitor let them grab the tutor & and fuck his suitor, she would blush, flush, flush, sush sush.......

Lying in bed was she, lying in life was she, stumbled upon years of experience, though , and through desertion , though. A doctor came to the rescue but she uglily declared that she was incurable. That was Priyanka for you who struck directly on to the dead's eyes and sometimes filled happiness with terror. She lived in the northern part of an unknown town of an unknown empire whose name people thought to take was a taboo. "No confidence in me", she would ask a passerby who didn't buy fruits from her. Priyanka sold dragon fruits that had a unique flavor and said to have aroused the feeling of love even amidst the evil of men. Men sometimes took her seriously . Though that was part of nature of men towards beauties....

The couples were ready to move in , lucky couples , a nice big house across the Heading street, awkward angle through the eyes , Rishabh was happy with Deepika or so he thought. Bookings were open for the monthly renting and Rishabh wanted to move in fast. Living in was the trend of the season and the couple didn't want to miss it . Mix your pace with Dr. Fixit and fix your relationship dude, the within screamed but Rishabh was not yet ready with a commitment, commitment issues saala..... same here same here .....

Was she dead by morning , that old hag who frowned at the dragon of the legends, bought on credit from the store, isn't that a dragon toy, oh it's the real dragon Ananya ....Ranveer didn't believe in the dragon story nor anything that Ananya said for he was lost into book of that lost ring or what was it? It was the outer ring's domino's pizza and Warren was quite happy with the investment ...have you played snakes and ladders with Charlie , a dragon in between the stairs would have been perfect. Ambiguity of talk was not something that neither Warren nor Charlie believed but Stan had a suggestion though , " go for the crazy ideas. What you got to loose" An iPhone maybe, lost and found in the pockets of God of cricket. He didn't mind being in the ad. He was having a chill of a time. How did he do it , hundreds of hundreds , ask Virat . But Virat was busy building the axe stairs where he could build a skyscraper of axes to almost wipe out the opposing forces . An event so smooth Virat wanted to celebrate within the bars of Naini prison. Time was short and a freezing winter across the border. James Achilees had already fallen love with the daughter of a Nizam but Sachin and Virat kind of controlled themselves not to fall prey to the mystic eyes of the sufi princess. He tried to lean into the burgeoning cement factory that was put under pressure to produce bagful of more cement into the construction of Sadiya bridge , at least Himanta was happy but not happy was Nicholas who had invested for the costs to come down. All for the social causes. Shahid and Virat kind of already infuriated with the Pehelgam incident took their axes to cut off their long held dreams of unity.

Anushka was drawing a circle and thinking about the radius. Does she think deep. Deep into the caves of the sadhus meditation. What did she like ? Priyanka's dragon fruits or Shahid and Virat's axes. That, only she could decide. She had a hangover last night out of partying in the Pattaya beach party. She wanted more though, a name added to the leaded, bedding onto the bedded. Anushka was short on beds for the refugees of Miyakistan where the war had gone on for nearly 6 years and there was no sign of stopping. Shahid had worn a cloak to fight the world war 2 while Virat was busy in the Indo China border, both doing their parts while Anushka was busy preparing a gold watch for Karan to travel to the times of Portugese invasion in India.

The year was a different one and weather matched in its difference. Language and regional rebellions were on the rise and student protests came out in large numbers . There were incidents of bloodshed in some places. Anushka couldn't keep herself in the oblivion . She joined the march only to save the bloodshed. Known to few, the bad elements sprang to action and created nuisance by pelting stones and engaging in violence in different parts. This time it was Anushka who came to the rescue......

Ranveer offered a cigarette to Virat under the shade of a tree and both of them smoked. Priyanka was plucking fruits by the sideways . She had a corner glance for both of them but chose to ignore the time travellers. Wait for the moment to ease into the snowfall. Wait for the burns to ease . Wait for Karan to arrive....

The water closet had a waterfall stored inside it and whoever opened it got that magical view . But it was a view who knew the secrets of the keyhole. Anushka was one such mystic. She sang and sang and bathed in the waterfall inside the water closet. People inside the house often wondered where did she wander off in the middle of day with her distant humming. A surprise of sorts, nature's gentle surprise off course.... Will you change the fortune of the Greeks once again, Shahid asked Anushka. Meet me at the Trafalgar square and bring out the edited documents from the Midday times where Devddutt wrote the article on Jaya. Sure...sure..... Rishabh had taken a new hobby of wearing a straw hat and painting the Hollywood posters black and blue pop hue. He did that at night just for fun . Fun without the sun. A computer geek by the day and billboard painter by the night. Deepika wasn't a bit satisfied. Where's the time to play ding dong,.., enough of ding dong , I have got so much of work....

Is the northern hill up the way to the house of Bill, that' s no way to fill, silly silly still, Virat's got a still photograph from the 50s when he returned from the Indo China war. That's where I belong . But the war is over . He laughed that demonic laughter and gulped a glass of beer in seconds...

Who's the Virgin lady over here? Priyanka giggled, who's the follower of Mary over here? Priyanka giggled again. After all he will see, see what , that you feel in the laps of a mafia don, that's it , Priyanka giggled again and ran to the fruit shop.

Sachin did have a self portrait in his house which he painted himself. Sachin didn't go near it and it was locked in his old store room ages ago. Ages ago, a group of sages came on his dream to talk him into painting his self portrait and he did so as soon as he woke up . But whenever he went near it a voice came inside his head that someday somehow that image would take his form in some kind of metamorphosis and become he. He suddenly became very afraid. Panicking, he packed the portrait and looked it in a safe cabinet in his store room. Some say some could hear Anushka humming the same tune when she bathed inside her house coming out melodiously from the store room . But Sachin refused to believe it. Perhaps he was in denial, who knows..........

His own memories, he can't outrun faster, Poonakon had a system for his madness. An attack on the artistic expression the people of Chabua said. Are we invited? To the lavish parties and soirees . Sorry that cannot be arranged. Indeed it was Poonakon 's place where only the survivors of trauma had a chance. Return to normalcy then . Only if you give me the chance . What you waiting for? Within speaking distance was a cuckoo bird who spoke about fate and food plate. People though had noticed her failure. Poonakon wasn't at all disturbed but took it on himself to prove. Hat shops were disappearing – I would look into that. My house not built- I would look into that . The water logging problem on the road- I would look into that. How much could Poonakon look into. Could he look into the future , could he agree with what fate had set up for him?

Stopped at the curtains, Isha wanted to burst some crackers but she was afraid of the sound, was supper over , Isha asked in a low tone, hush shush, we gotta catch Ranveer red handed, nervous with laughter she kissed her mother. The television was showing some dramatic serials about saas bahu and the intricacies involved , would you be involved in that , no no, let the living room be free , purification of air, Nisaba would handle the air freshner products, let Isha burn some crackers, after all it's Diwali. No no the air quality is poor and aam admi would hate it . But are they ruling ? Who ruled anyways....

The tarot card had a message for him , stay away from uttering a word , how is that possible, not even one, not even sign language, no , perhaps for consolation a spittoon cup but nothing more. Then reflect on what was wrong , are you hungry, eat some curd that too from Amul, it's a cooperative society so cooperate....let the fashion fekus seek the stars but you be truthful, I will I will....

In case Anushka needed to converse with Avni who was still in district 9 and working with the homeless she would catch the coast nearby and fly away . Telepathy is a thing already known to dogs , an official copy yet not received . Tiger was about to close his eyes for the fight was too long and tiresome when Priyanka fed him some water. An outbreak of the plague was what these survivors of death (immortal ones as some would say) would fear. Darkness in East company's demands was what they worried a lot. A halo of majesty in the Mughal kings was what Virat hated the most. Karan still busy on the working of the hidden watch on the tower of Pisa smiled at the distraction. A few days earlier Tiger finally breaking out of hundred years of sleep had spoke to Shahid about the construction of Sadiya bridge. Shahid did complete it and Tiger could finally rest for a bit.

Who had more guile they asked. It wasn't that Anant hadn't heard of the word before or hadn't been beguiled before. Sophie did that for Anant many times before. She had that craft for sure but whether she had the craft to recognize Kraft as an investment was another question. As for questions Anant was rather busy answering Meg lanning postures. What do I speak of this midnight child. She had that kinky drama with her curling lips for sure. Do the labels identify with her? Do the labels enjoy and party with her often! "Does she feel lonely sometimes? Are the blends of butterscotch enough for her? Anant would be satisfied. It feels the lonely tune of numbness gratifies itself. The anger on the field satisfies itself. Is the anger on something draws someone? Is he the one? Is he the only one? He's just a speck of dust among the billions. Why would Ecclestone care in the world, why would they have the least care in the world about the scarred one? What's the thinking anyways? It's no Alice in Wonderland to fall into a rabbit hole. And Meg's not Matilda to read the rubbish rhymes. Sophie's not Alice to be his queen of the fairyland.

None is there to be conquered and none is the conqueror. It's not a history lesson nor an engrossing story...

"No wonder! You're like a wonder woman..." was the talk between Ranveer and Alissa Healy. Healy could have been easily healed off her torturous chamber and career at theatres on those kind words of Ranveer. Ranveer had dressed casually that day, too casual some would say that he visited her in chappals i.e. sandals. Those were not of sandalwood but of rubber and had an elegant aroma that the receptionist at the restaurant immediately took notice of. She immediately denied their entry pointing out his sandals as a cause of concern for the elite community that they served. Alyssa anyways had played lot of elite and bold and rich characters on stage and she was almost put off by their sight. She loved Ranveer not because he was a struggler in the art scene but he was so soaking. As if he could soak all her worries in. They weren't worried about not getting the entry at the restaurant. They went to the subway stand and started biting on the sandwiches at the nearby park. The ducks were fading infront of them into the small beautiful pond. Suddenly Ranveer panicked about something. Alyssa being concerned asked what it was. He said, he had forgotten how to draw ducks and ponds. It had been a long time since he had drawn any. He had been so busy painting the vibes of abstracts that he forgot about the nature. And it now scared him seeing the beautiful ducks in water. Alyssa tried to calm him and rested his head on her chest and both relaxed amidst the playing ducks and the evaporating pond in the summer.

Could you see from the air, or smell the land and then trade the wind

"Oh! I come for the trade of spices"

"Speuzes what's sat"

"Spices !!The far reaching aromatic Indian spices"

"Along with that I bring to you the time lusty, busty and the rusty whores of Bombay Burmah side, Ishapuri and Ananyavali, virgin, hot, sensuous, but fiery, both upper and the later."

The fight was about to start in the coliseum and Prince Harry was busy drinking his booze and looking at the tits of Isha and Ananya

"The winner gets these hot tits"

The crowd roared in approval.

Isha and Ananya stood silent, reserved and without burning a sweat went through the whole ordeal. Russel Crow was a great fighter. He would fight lions and tigers with the same ease as humans. This time there were twelve men with arms and it took five minutes to do the job. Russel wasn't breathing heavily and after the victory bowed in front of the emperor.

The emperor gave him the tits.

Russel took home the tits.

There was nothing much to adore in the house of Russel Crow. He was a fighter with little necessities outside war.

"Water", Russel asked Isha as he took off his bandage off his hand and Isha who was all handcuffed and looking nice and beautiful.

"Russel, there's a war, a world war & you can only save the world"

To which even Ananya joined in. "The Gods have conspired to have the furher killed in your hands"

"Huh! Gods" Russel laughed a bid indignantly while washing his face.

"Haven't you read the letter"

Isha and Ananya were confused.

"Why Am I an Atheist, by Bhagat Singh"

"Anyway how's the trial going on"

"Bhagat would escape. Let him play his part. But right now you must move to Germany, 1943."

"Oh that's an interesting time, isn't it? I just hope Karan finds his timepiece...."